Enid Blyton's
NODDY
and Martha Monkey

BBC BOOKS

It had been a messy day in Toyland. Noddy and his car were very tired and dirty from helping Farmer Straw in his fields.

"Oh dear," said Noddy to his car, yawning loudly, "I'm so tired and hungry, but I must wash you before the mud sets all hard."

Just then Martha Monkey appeared.
"Hello, Noddy," she said. "What a dirty car!"
    "It's been working very hard,"
said Noddy, crossly.
    "Then you must give its face a
good scrub and mind you wash
behind its ears!" laughed
Martha Monkey rudely.

3

"That silly monkey," said Noddy, as Martha Monkey left. "She makes me feel tireder than ever." With that, he slid, yawning, down the side of the car, and would have fallen fast asleep if Master Tubby Bear from next door hadn't chosen that very moment to appear.

"Ooh, Noddy, isn't your car dirty!" said Tubby. "May I wash it?"

"No, thank you. You'll probably do something naughty," said Noddy.

"Please, Noddy," begged Master Tubby Bear. "I promise to be good."

"All right," said Noddy. "Wash the car then, but be very careful! If you do it really well, I will take you for a ride."

"Oh, thank you, Noddy!" Master Tubby Bear moved forward to hug Noddy, but in his excitement, he knocked Noddy over instead.

Mrs Tubby Bear arrived just at that moment, carrying a cake on a plate. "Yoohoo! Noddy! I've baked you one of my special ginger cakes."

"Thank you so much," said Noddy, yawning. "I'm terribly hungry."

"And you look so tired!" said Mrs Tubby Bear. "Come inside and have some tea, while Master Tubby cleans your car. He's trying very hard to be a good and helpful bear."

The next morning, Noddy found his car standing gleaming in the driveway.

"Good morning, little car," he said. "You do look clean and smart! Master Tubby Bear really did give you a very good wash."

But when Noddy tried to start the car, it gave a few splutters, jerked forwards and then ground to a halt.

Just then Big-Ears arrived. "Oh, Big-Ears, something
dreadful has happened to my car!
Listen," said Noddy, as he tried
to start the car again.

The car jerked up and down,
spluttered once or twice
and then stopped.

"That car has hiccups!" said Big-Ears. "Have you put something funny in the petrol tank?"

"No, I haven't, but naughty Tubby Bear washed my car. Perhaps he may have done."

"Come along," said Big-Ears. "Let's look in your garage."

In the garage Big-Ears found a pile
of empty ginger-beer bottles.

"Surely that naughty Tubby Bear
didn't fill my petrol tank with
ginger beer!" said Noddy.

But he had. Mrs Tubby
Bear sent her naughty son
to his room for the day, while
Noddy and Big-Ears took
the car to Mr Sparks' garage
to be mended.

At the garage Mr Sparks shook his head and said, "Tsk, tsk, that car will have to stay here while I clean it out."

"But without my car to give people rides," said Noddy, "I won't be able to earn anything!"

"Don't worry, Noddy," said Big-Ears. "I will lend you my bicycle and we will tie on the little cart behind it."

"And I have a job for you," said Mr Sparks. "You can go to the station and collect a pair of new tyres for me."

"You are so kind," said Noddy. "I could hug you both!"

Noddy collected Big-Ears' bike and cart and then picked up the tyres from the station.

"I do miss my little car!" he said, as he cycled back to the garage. "This is very hard work, and those tyres are so heavy!"

Noddy was so busy pedalling along that he didn't
notice Martha Monkey sitting on a gate, until she called
out to him, "Hello, Noddy! What's happened to your car?
Is it too dirty to be driven?"

"I'm too busy to talk to you, Martha Monkey," said
Noddy, cycling past, puffing and panting. As he reached
the top of the hill, one of the tyres rolled off Big-Ears' cart.
Martha Monkey called after him to stop, but Noddy
wouldn't listen.

"How silly Noddy is," said Martha Monkey. "Why, I'll take this tyre to Mr Sparks myself."

She picked up the tyre and began bowling it along the road like a hoop.

But soon the tyre ran away from Martha Monkey and went rolling down the road towards Toy Town.

"Come back, you naughty tyre, come back!" cried
Martha Monkey, giving chase, as the tyre rolled away
from her downhill.

Noddy cycled through the main street of Toy Town, unaware that the tyre was close behind him. It hit Mr Wobbly Man and almost knocked him over.

"Now then, what's going on here?" said Mr Plod, getting out his notebook.

But the tyre rolled on.

Through the town square it rolled, knocking the Skittle family flying. The little Skittles laughed and shrieked with glee, as they loved being knocked over.

The tyre rolled on into the café. Mr Sparks and the Clockwork Mouse ran away to escape it. The tyre rolled out again into the market square.

Martha Monkey was just asking
Dinah Doll if she had seen the
tyre, when it came up behind
her and sent her running
away down the road.

"Oh dear, oh dear," shrieked Martha Monkey, racing along like the wind.

Soon after, Noddy arrived at the garage and was
amazed to find that he had only one tyre on his cart.
"You must have lost the other tyre, Noddy," said
Mr Sparks. "I'm afraid that you'll have to pay for it."

"But I still haven't earned any money," said Noddy, in despair. "Oh, what shall I do?"

Just then Martha Monkey came running up with the tyre following close behind her.

"Noddy! Noddy!" she called. "I've brought your tyre!"

"Well done both of you!" said Mr Sparks. "You shall each have sixpence."

"And Noddy," Mr Sparks continued, "your car is mended."

"Oh, thank you, Mr Sparks!" said Noddy. "And thank you, Martha Monkey, for helping me. You can have a ride in my car, if you like."

"All right," said Martha Monkey. "If you want me to – and if you are sure it's working properly!"

With Martha Monkey beside him, Noddy drove his clean, shiny car through the countryside.

"I quite like your car, after all," said Martha.

"Parp! Parp!" went the little car contentedly.

Other Noddy *TV Tie-in titles*
available from BBC Children's Books

Noddy and his Bell
Noddy and the Goblins
Noddy and the Kite
Noddy Loses Sixpence
Noddy and the Naughty Tail
Noddy and his New Friend
Noddy and the Pouring Rain

Other TV Tie-in titles in preparation

Noddy and the Broken Bicycle
Noddy Delivers Some Parcels
Noddy Gets a New Job
Noddy and the Milkman
Noddy and the Special Key

Published by BBC Books
a division of BBC Enterprises Limited
Woodlands, 80 Wood Lane, London W12 0TT
First published 1993
Text and stills copyright © BBC Enterprises Limited 1993
ISBN 0 563 36861 6

Based on the Television series, produced by Cosgrove Hall Productions, inspired by the Noddy Books
which are copyright © Darrell Waters Limited 1949-1968

Enid Blyton's signature and Noddy are Trademarks of Darrell Waters Limited

Typeset in 17/21 pt Garamond by BBC Books

Printed and bound in Great Britain by Cambus Limited, East Kilbride
Colour separations by DOT Gradations, Chelmsford
Cover printed by Cambus Limited, East Kilbride